THE MONSTER IS COMING!

Paul Shipton

Illustrated by Sholto Walker

Chapter 1

It was a Monday morning. The village children were all at school. Simon was looking dreamily out of the window.

Suddenly Simon heard a shout. "Run! Hide!"
someone cried.

The children looked out of the window.
People were running away. Some people
were shouting. They all looked afraid.

A woman ran into the school.

"Run!" she shouted. "Hide! There's a monster in the village! It'll eat us! It'll crush us in our homes!"

"Don't be silly!" said the teacher.

Then they heard the booming sound of giant footsteps. A huge monster, as tall as a tree, stamped past their school. It shook its giant, hairy head from side to side and roared loudly.

"We should hide in the village hall,"
said the teacher sensibly. "Line up in the
school playground."

The playground was full of people. Somehow,
Simon lost the teacher.

Simon was afraid, but he wanted to see what was going on. It's not often you see a monster in your village! The monster was going towards the village square. Simon followed it.

There were lots of villagers in the
village square. The monster was sitting in
the middle of the square. It was still
roaring loudly.

The villagers were half afraid, but half angry too.

"Who does this monster think it is?" asked one man angrily. The villagers shook their fists.

"We should chase it away!" shouted a woman. They picked up a long log.

"One, two, three . . . charge!"

The villagers charged. The monster gave
an even louder roar. The roar was so loud
it blew them over.

"It might want something to eat," said
the village baker.

He filled a tub with bread and cakes.
A few villagers took the tub to the monster.
Then they ran away quickly.

The monster picked up some cakes
and started to eat them. Then it started
roaring again.

"Why is he roaring? I make *good* cakes!"
said the baker angrily.

"The monster might be too cold," said an old man. So the villagers made a fire.

"It will be warm now," said the old man.

Chapter 2

The monster roared again. The roar was so loud it blew the fire out.

"What now?" asked the villagers.

Nobody knew what to do. Then Simon had an idea. He picked up a stick and ran into the square.

"Come back!" a man shouted.

"Stop him!" shouted an old woman.

It was too late. Simon ran towards
the monster. Simon used the stick to draw a
picture on the dusty ground. It was a picture
of a boy. The monster just looked at him.

First Simon pointed to the boy. Then he
pointed to himself. He said his name
loudly, "Simon."

The monster nodded. It understood.

Next, Simon drew a much bigger picture
on the ground. It was a picture of the
monster. Simon pointed to the picture,
and then to the monster. At last the
monster spoke.

"BLOG," said the monster. Simon smiled
and nodded, because he understood.
Its name was Blog!

Suddenly, the monster picked up a big log.
It drew a picture of a monster, but this one
was even bigger. It was huge. The monster
pointed at this picture sadly. Then it began
to roar even louder.

All at once, Simon understood. The monster was roaring because it wanted someone!

"Of course!" he shouted to the villagers. "It's not angry — it's lost!"

"But what should we do?" asked one villager.

"We should get it to roar even louder," said Simon. "Then another monster might hear it."

"How can we do that?" asked another villager.

Simon stood close to the monster. Then Simon roared and roared as loudly as he could. The monster looked puzzled.

Then it began to roar. It roared so loudly that the hats blew off the villagers.

Then it roared even more loudly so the leaves blew off the trees!

Then it roared more loudly still, so the curtains blew out of the houses.

Suddenly, there was a boom in the distance. The ground shook. Then there was another louder boom.

Something was coming, and it was big. Suddenly, the square was dark. Something was blocking the sunlight.

A giant monster stepped into the village.
It was careful not to crush any homes
under its huge feet.

The smaller monster looked up and started to laugh. The giant monster picked up the smaller monster with one huge hand.

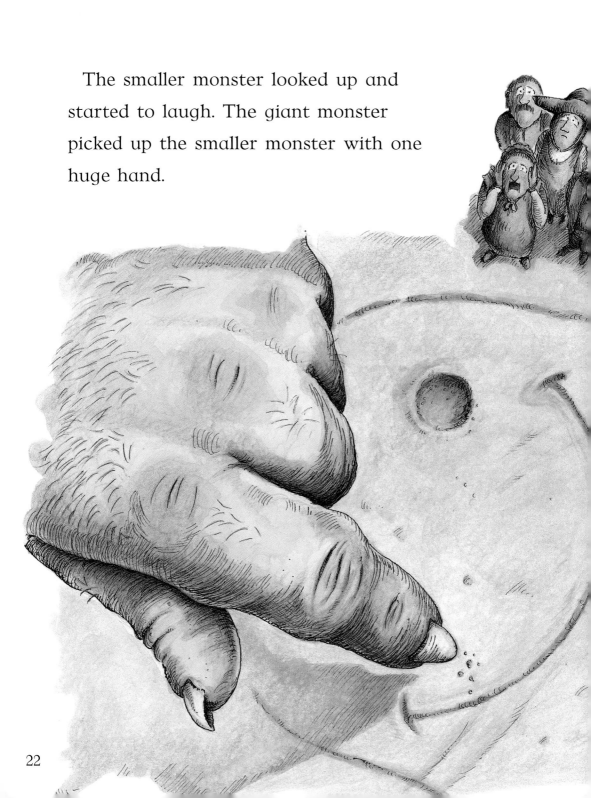

Then the giant monster bent down and started to draw. It drew a smile on the picture of the big monster.

Simon understood. The monster had found its child. He looked up at the little monster and smiled.

Then the two monsters stamped off towards the mountains.